# Shake the Hand, Bite the Taco

# Shake the Hand, Bite the Taco

## Jeff MacNelly

St. Martin's Press          New York

Library of Congress Cataloging-in-Publication Data

MacNelly, Jeff.
  Shake the hand, bite the taco / Jeff MacNelly.
    p.  cm.
  ISBN 0-312-03931-X
  I. Title.
PN6728.S475M335   1990
791.5'973—dc20                                                    89-27131
                                                                      CIP

First Edition
10  9  8  7  6  5  4  3  2

# Shake the Hand, Bite the Taco

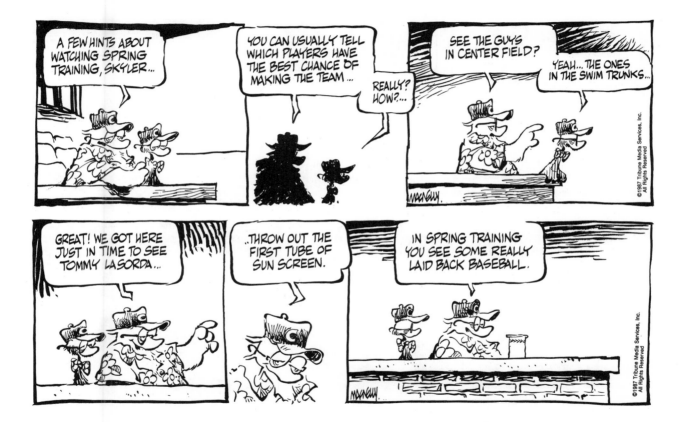

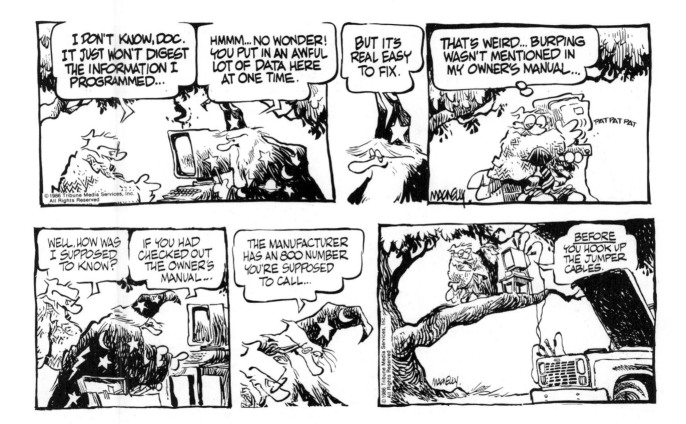

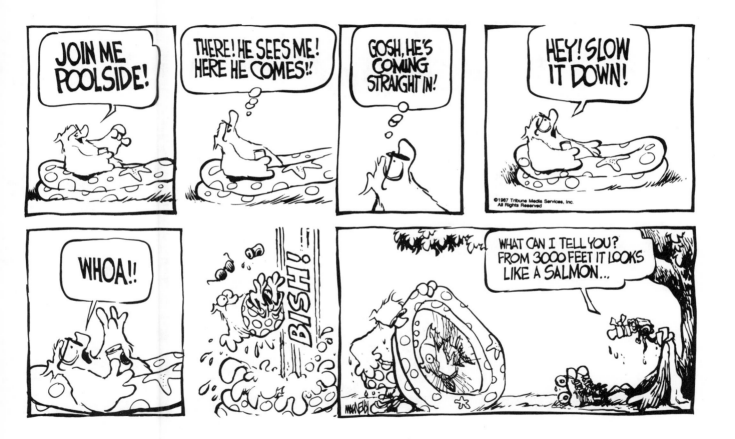

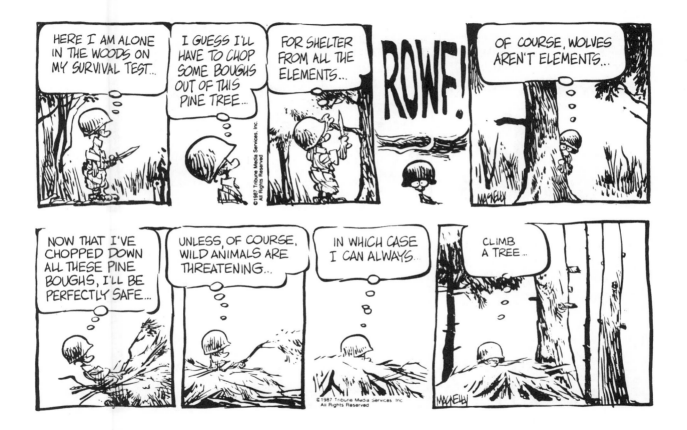

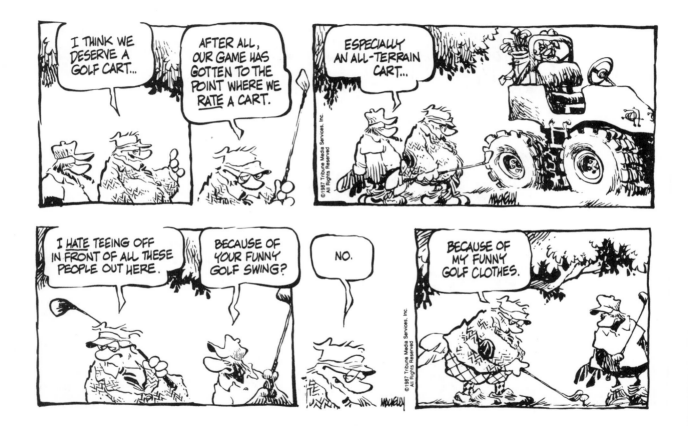

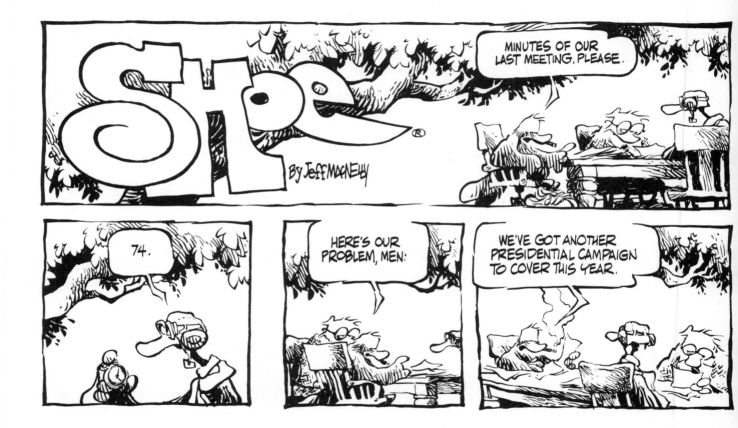

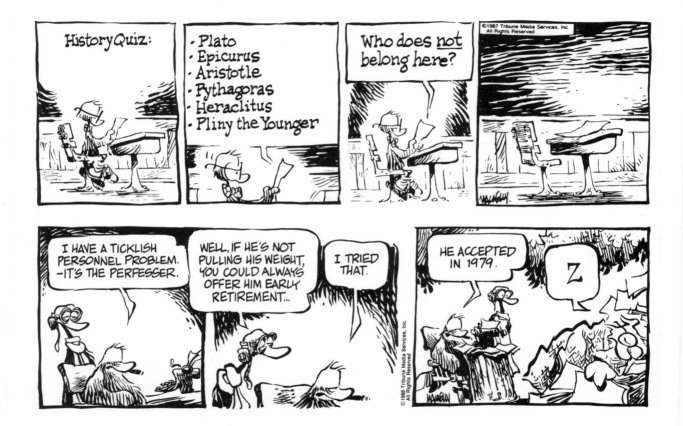

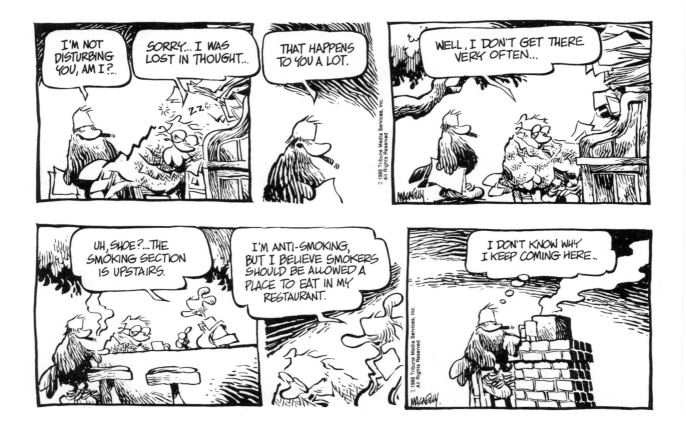

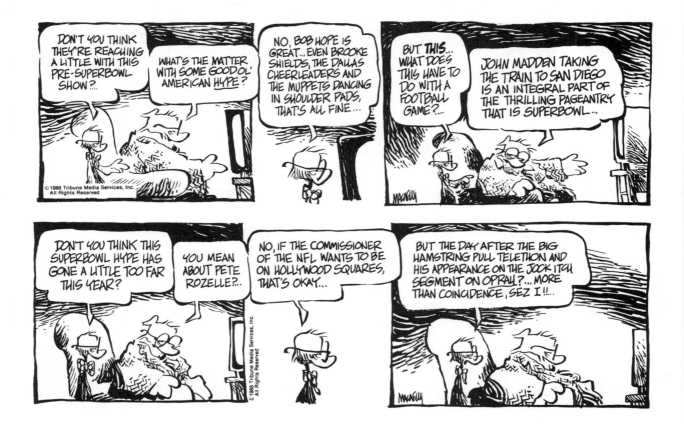

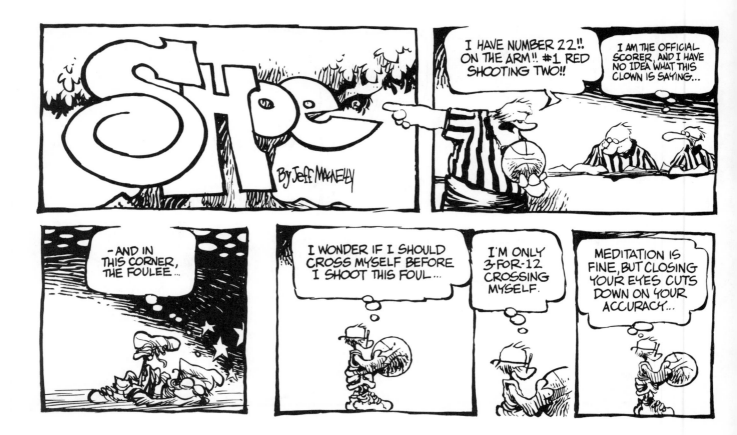

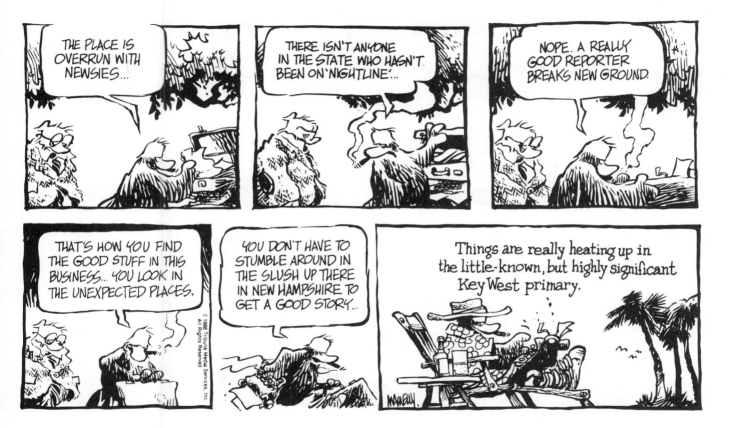

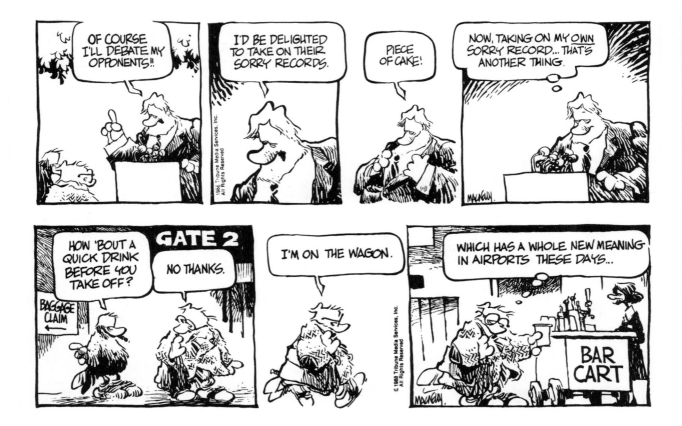

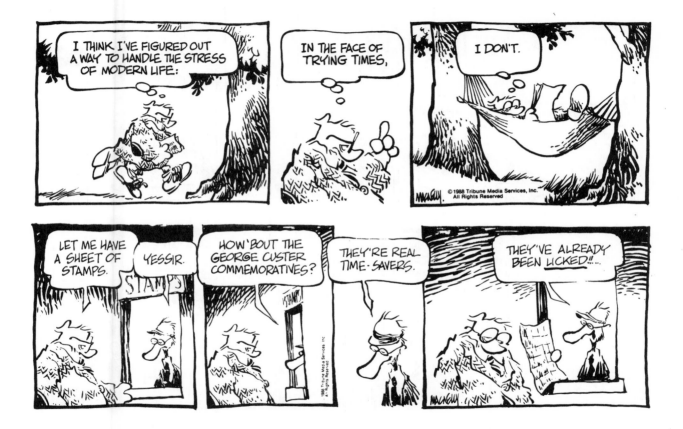

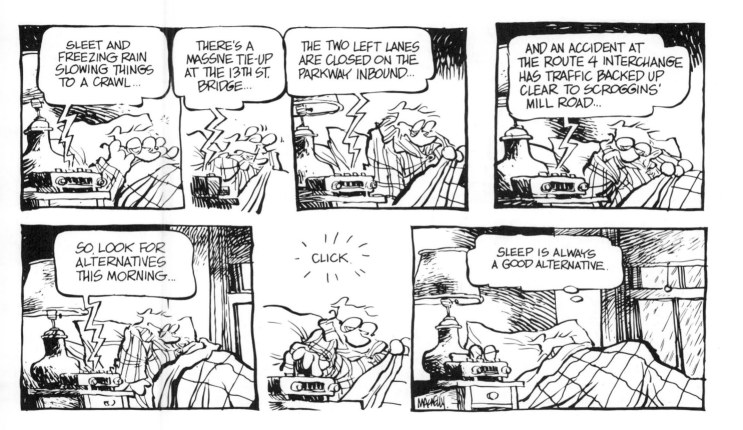

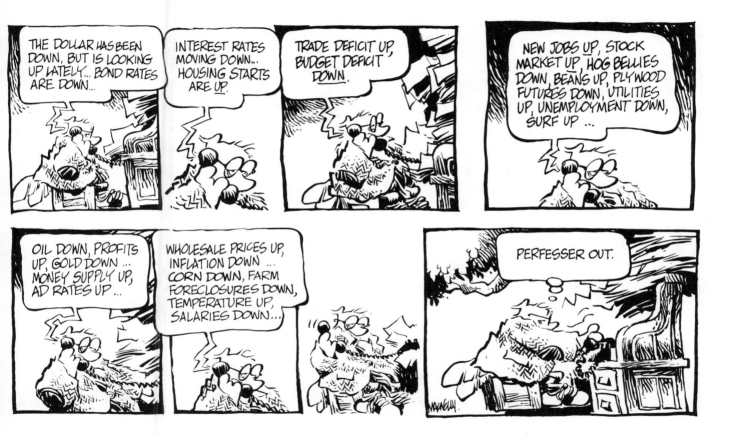

"Anyone who likes journalism, wry humor, cigars, good drawing or birds will almost certainly find that this Shoe always fits," wrote the *Washington Post* in reviewing the first collection of SHOE comic strips, drawn by three-time Pulitzer Prize winner Jeff MacNelly of the *Chicago Tribune*.

MacNelly began the comic strip, which appears in more than 1,000 newspapers, daily and Sunday, in 1977. He won his first Pulitzer Prize in 1972, his second in 1978 and a third in 1985 for his editorial cartoons. He has also won the George Polk Award and twice received the Reuben, the highest honor of The National Cartoonists Society.

A native of Cedarhurst, New York, who attended Phillips Academy of Andover, Massachusetts, MacNelly began his career drawing sports and editorial cartoons for his college paper, the *Daily Tar Heel*, at the University of North Carolina. Later, as editorial cartoonist for the town newspaper, *The Chapel Hill Weekly*, MacNelly hit his stride, spoofing the local upheavals and "ridculosities" that characterize North Carolina politics.

His efforts earned the National Newspaper Association's 1969 award for best editorial cartooning, and the following year he became editorial cartoonist for the Richmond, Virginia, *News Leader*. In March 1982, he joined the *Chicago Tribune*.

MacNelly currently resides in Washington, D.C.

Copies of Jeff MacNelly's previous books are available from your local bookstore, or you can order them directly from St. Martin's Press by returning this coupon with a check or money order to:

St. Martin's Press
175 Fifth Avenue
New York, NY 10010
ATTN: Cash Sales Department

For bulk order (25 copies or more) for resale, fund-raising, etc., please call the St. Martin's Press Special Sales Department toll-free at (800) 221-7945 for information about special discounts. In New York State, call (212) 674-5151

Please send me _____ copy(ies) of *Too Old for Summer Camp and Too Young to Retire* (312-01822-3) @ $5.95 each.                                            $ _____
Please send me _____ copy(ies) of *A Cigar Means Never Having to Say You're Sorry* (312-02651-X) @ $5.95 each.                                            $ _____
Postage & handling ($1.50 for first copy + $.75 for each additional copy)      $ _____
Total enclosed                                                                 $ _____

Name _____

Street Address_____

City _____ State _____ Zip_____